CONTENTS

Chapter 1

The man sitting behind the big walnut desk was about 70 years old and grossly overweight. His huge, drooping mustache reminded Nikki of a walrus raising his head out of the sea. All that was lacking were the tusks.

Nikki Peters was applying for a job as his personal secretary. She'd been drawn to the job ad by two things: The pay was outstanding and the work was described as "unique and challenging." At 24, with no relationship going and a bank job that had become boring, Nikki was ready for something challenging.

"I have outstanding computer skills," Nikki told Hal Dempsey. "I can handle just about anything that comes up."

"Good," Mr. Dempsey said, his

mustache twitching, "but what I must know is—is there a detective hiding somewhere in your soul?"

Nikki didn't know exactly how to answer him. "I'm curious and logical. I think I'd be good at investigation," she said finally, wondering what his strange question was all about.

"Well, here's the situation. I have two sons. Dylan is the eldest. He's already in the business with me. I've made my fortune in mattresses, you know."

Nikki did know. Before applying for this job she had done some research on Mr. Dempsey. He was the founder of the Royal Mattress Company, comfy mattress makers to the world. The company offered whatever anyone could need—split mattresses to accommodate a hard and softer side, mattresses designed especially for bad backs, floating-on-air mattresses—whatever. It was even rumored that the Royal Mattress Company had supplied custom-made beds to the White House and to Buckingham Palace in England.

"Yes, I know that you make fine mattresses," Nikki said.

"Not fine—the *best*," Mr. Dempsey said proudly. Then he frowned. "But my younger son, Colin, has never wanted any part of the business. Can you believe it? I'm seriously thinking of disinheriting him completely and leaving everything to Dylan."

"I see," Nikki said, wondering what her role in this would be.

"Colin is a wastrel—a disrespectful bum. He's never done a blasted thing I asked him to do. Now I think he might be a criminal as well. Ms. Peters, I need you to find out once and for all what that little beast is up to. I want you to worm your way into his life and give me the real scoop. It's only fair to get all the facts before I decide to tear up his birth certificate and deny him as my son," Mr. Dempsey said.

Nikki had felt a tremor of concern at hearing the word *criminal*. "What kind of criminal behavior do you suspect him of?" she asked.

"Swindling, I'm sorry to say. I've been told he's involved in some scheme to defraud elderly people. Nothing violent, but a despicable plot to hornswoggle poor old folks who aren't as swift as they used to be," Mr. Dempsey said. Obviously, he didn't think that *he* fit into the category of an older person not as smart as he once was. Then, as if reading Nikki's mind, Mr. Dempsey sneered smugly and said, "Remember, miss—I said *poor* old folks. A man who's become as successful as I have never loses his edge!"

Nikki smiled, wondering if Mr. Dempsey would offer her this unusual job. If so, she was ready to take it. Suddenly, the man leaned forward. "May I call you Nikki?" he asked.

"Oh yes, of course," Nikki said.

"Very good. And I insist that you call me Hal. All my employees do," Mr. Dempsey said with a smile and a nod.

So Nikki was hired. But she still wasn't sure why she had been chosen until he said, "I've interviewed about ten young women for this job. I must tell you that Colin is kind of—a *collector* of young women—but only the most charming and lovely. Quite frankly, no other applicant combined beauty and intelligence quite as well as you."

Nikki blushed. "Why, thank you, Mr. Demp—er—Hal," she said with a smile.

A few minutes later Nikki left the highrise office and walked to her Corolla. She was carrying an attaché case filled with information about Colin Dempsey. She didn't look at any of it until she was comfortably settled back home in her condo. She had bought the place just last year. As an executive secretary at the bank, she'd been making a good salary. When a good deal on some new condos had come up, she jumped on it.

That was about the same time Nikki broke off her two-year relationship with Bart Wheeler. It was on New Year's Eve that Bart had finally had the guts to tell her the truth. He said that although he loved dating her, marriage had never been an option. Nikki had gone home that night and cried herself to sleep. All along she'd felt sure that she and Bart would be married one day. Then it was all over between them—just like that.

Nikki soon decided that she wasn't wasting anymore time on a relationship that was going nowhere. So she had called it off. Now at long last she felt she was pretty much over Bart.

She settled down in her recliner and opened the attaché case. Sipping a cup of coffee, she started her research by looking at several pictures of Colin.

He was a handsome guy.

"Wow!" Nikki said aloud, startling the Persian cat at her feet. The guy was fantastic! He looked like a movie or TV star—broad-shouldered, dark-haired and dark-eyed, a smile that would light up any room. How, Nikki wondered, did a guy who looked like a walrus have a son who looked like that? Maybe, she thought, the mother was attractive. Yeah. The mother must have passed her good-looking genes on to her son.

Then Nikki read through Colin's college record. As far as grades went, he'd never done better than a C. In the end, he'd flunked out of two good Ivy League universities. Then he'd been in the army but was eventually kicked out for fighting with an officer. Mr. Dempsey had added a note on this page. It said that he had "forced" his son into the military, hoping in vain that it would make a man out of him.

A string of small-time jobs followed, all short term. He'd been a fry cook, a parking lot attendant, a clerk in a deli, and he had done some telemarketing.

Nikki looked at the next page. It was a brief report from a detective agency that Mr. Dempsey must have hired last summer.

"At this time Mr. Colin Dempsey is selling a line of overpriced vitamins and other questionable health products to senior citizens. And he's apparently making false claims about the benefits."

Nikki closed the file and finished her coffee. She sat there for a few moments, digesting all the information. Then she glanced through a stack of the Dempsey family's snapshots.

Dylan was a nice-looking fellow too, but not nearly as handsome as Colin. And just as she had thought, their mother *was* a beautiful woman.

"What happened to Colin?" Nikki asked herself, trying to remember some of her psychology classes in college. Maybe the younger son felt he was being forced into a mold. It would be no surprise if he rebelled against that.

Maybe that was all that was wrong with him. In that case he wasn't as awful as his father seemed to think.

The file contained Colin's current phone number and address. Nikki saw that he lived downtown in a tacky neighborhood. She knew the area. Most of the stores there were boarded up. The apartment buildings were run down, and there were big cracks in the sidewalks. The make and license number of Colin's car were also listed.

The very next morning, Nikki drove over to Colin's apartment building. She spotted his old Sunfire parked on the street. Good—he was home! She parked across the street and read the newspaper, waiting for him to come out.

Before long a young man who looked like Colin emerged from the building. Nikki saw him heading toward the Sunfire. The guy looked terrible—sick, almost—and seemed to be unsteady on his feet. Then Nikki realized what the problem was. Colin was drunk. She watched him fumble in his pocket for his car keys and then drop them in the street. When he tried to pick them up, he staggered and nearly fell.

Nikki jumped out of her car and ran across the street.

Chapter 2

Nikki wasn't thinking about her job when she dashed across the street. A very drunk man was about to drive off in his car: Her reaction was automatic. She saw it as her *duty* to stop him. Nikki could never forget that her own father had been killed by a drunk driver when she was just five years old.

"Hey, mister, you're in no condition to drive!" Nikki called out as Colin again dropped his keys in an effort to unlock the car door.

Bleary-eyed, Colin looked up and stared at her. "Huh? Who're you?" he asked in a slurred voice.

"Never mind who I am. You can't drive that car when you're as drunk as you are," Nikki said.

"Sure I can," he said with a glassy smile, as he finally opened the car door.

Impulsively, Nikki reached out and snatched the car keys from his hand.

"*Heyyyy!*" he protested. "You wan' me to get fired? I gotta go to work."

"Get in the passenger side," Nikki said pleasantly but forcefully. "I'll take you to a fast food place and get you a big cup of coffee. I'll drive."

Colin stared at her blankly. "Who *are* you?" he asked in confusion. But he got in the passenger side without an argument. Nikki was glad that he didn't seem to be a mean or violent drunk. But the smell of liquor on his breath was overpowering.

Nikki drove the Sunfire about two blocks before she found a drive-through fast food place. She ordered two coffees and parked on the street. "Here, drink this," she said.

"Nah. I don' need any coffee," he mumbled. But he took the cup and started drinking from it anyway.

"My name is Nikki Peters," Nikki said. "I was just passing by when I saw that you were in no condition to drive. I'm sorry to interfere. But it really scares me when I see a drunk person taking the wheel. I lost my dad to a drunk driver when I was real young."

"I'm not drunk," Colin said in a slightly sobered voice. "Man, it's only eight o'clock in the morning! How could I be drunk already?"

"It's almost *ten* o'clock—and you're drunk enough," Nikki insisted. "If a cop saw you driving the way you are, you'd get hit with a DUI. And if you were really lucky, you'd only have to pay a big fine. If you *weren't* lucky, you could smash up your car and get hurt or killed—and maybe kill somebody else."

Colin Dempsey took a deep breath and let out a moan. "My head hurts. I can't go to work." Then he looked down at himself. He wore dirty jeans and a sweatshirt stained with orange juice. The deep yellow stain nearly covered up the Aztec football logo.

"I'll drive you home," Nikki offered.

"I guess you might as well," he said.

Nikki followed Colin up the stairs to his apartment. This was all working out even better than she had expected. She'd been wondering how she could break the ice and get into this man's life. Now it would be easy. On the way up the stairs, Colin faltered once or twice even though he was gripping the railing. When it looked like he might fall, Nikki steadied him.

Inside the messy, dark apartment, Colin sat down at the kitchen table. He put his face in his hands and muttered, "Everything is all screwed up. . . . It's all screwed up."

Nikki looked in the refrigerator. It was mostly filled with beer, but she finally found six eggs. Then, in a bottom cupboard, she found a dirty skillet and wiped it out with a paper towel. With some effort she finally got one of the dirty burners on the stove to work. The pilot light had blown out.

"I'm scrambling some eggs," Nikki said. "They'll make you feel better." Nikki was proud of herself. Her boast to Mr. Dempsey hadn't been exaggerated. She *could* handle most everything that came up. Bart Wheeler would never know what a great woman he could have married. "Stupid fool," Nikki now thought. "He didn't deserve me."

Colin looked up and squinted at her. "Who are you again?" he asked.

"My name is Nikki Peters," she said, scrambling the eggs until they were light and fluffy. She wished she had some grated cheese to put on them. Then the eggs would be perfect. But that was too much to hope for in this place.

"What are you doing here?" Colin asked. "Did we go out last night?"

"No. I was just passing by when I

saw that you were drunk. I stopped you from driving off in your car," Nikki said. She put a plate of scrambled eggs before Colin. Then she started to look for silverware. She let out a gasp. There was a pistol in the drawer. "Hey, there's a *gun* in here!" she said in a shaky voice.

Colin sprang to his feet. He was still unsteady, but he appeared to be sobering up fast. He looked at Nikki and said, "You better go now."

"Why do you have a gun?" Nikki asked. "It's dangerous to leave guns lying around the house—especially when somebody gets drunk."

"I need it for my work. I'm, uh—a security guard, you know. Hey, thanks for everything, but you'd better go now," Colin said.

"You won't try to drive off again, will you?" Nikki asked.

"No. Please just go," he said.

"I'm just trying to help you. Why don't you eat some of your eggs before they're cold?" Nikki said. Now that she had her foot in the door, she didn't want to leave until she had to. She'd already confirmed much of what Hal Dempsey suspected: Colin was a bum. He lived like a bum and he looked like a bum. Worse yet, he appeared to be a *drunken* bum. That wasn't good—and Nikki doubted the security guard story. Most security guards didn't carry guns. And anyway—what reputable company would entrust its security to this man?

Colin sat down at the table and started eating the eggs. Nikki felt sorry for the guy. He was really pathetic. Only 28 years old and living in a rathole like this—stumbling around drunk at 9:30 in the morning!

Nikki sat across the table from Colin. She wondered why Mr. Dempsey didn't seem to be worried about his son's health. His only question was whether or not Colin should be disinherited. His concern was all about money.

"You'd think Mr. Dempsey would want to help the guy," Nikki thought to herself. "After all, this is his *son*."

Colin finished the eggs. He looked kind of gaunt—as if he hadn't been eating regularly. He drank another cup of the coffee that Nikki had brewed. Then he said, "I'm going to lie down now. I've got a terrible headache. Thanks for all your help, but I've got to get some sleep. My head hurts a lot."

Nikki watched him shuffle into the tiny living room. He flopped down on the couch, fully clothed. In a few minutes he was sleeping.

"Wow," Nikki thought, "here I am in this man's seedy apartment—a guy I don't even know. Was I crazy to leave the bank? My job as an executive secretary wasn't so bad. I could have stayed there for the rest of my working life. Twenty years from now I'd have built up a nice 401K, and I could do what all retired ladies do—travel around the world on cruises."

But Nikki *had* to quit the bank. Bart Wheeler worked there, too. After they had broken up, they kept running into each other on the elevators and in the halls. Bart was always polite. Sometimes he'd be talking intimately with a pretty young girl. No, she was right to get out of there. Seeing Bart hurt so much that Nikki dreaded every day. One by one, her warm memories had turned bitter. Nikki knew she had to start over some place else. But what kind of a trade-off was this? Here she was in a loser's crummy apartment, watching him passed out in a drunken sleep.

Suddenly the front door opened. A short, dirty guy had let himself in with a key! An awful scar divided the man's forehead into two segments. Nikki couldn't help staring. It looked like somebody had tried to cut his head in two with an axe.

The man glared at her. "What're you

doing here, lady?" he growled.

Nikki's heart began to pound. When she tried to speak, her voice came out high-pitched and squeaky. She would have run out the door if the scarred stranger hadn't been blocking her escape route.

Chapter 3

"I just met Mr. Dempsey when he was—uh—about to drive away, and he was—sick—so I helped him," Nikki said.

The man went over to the couch where Colin was sleeping. He gave him a rough shake. "What's goin' on here? Who's the babe?" he demanded.

Nikki didn't know what to do. She tried to calm herself. Was it likely that she was in any *real* danger from this grungy-looking man? Probably not. She hesitated. After all, it was her job to learn as much as possible about Colin. Maybe this guy could help her out.

"What?" Colin muttered as he stretched up from the couch.

"I said, there's a babe here, man!" the scarred man yelled at him. "Who is she

THE CASE OF THE BAD SEED

and what's she doing here?"

Colin blinked and shook his head as if to clear out the cobwebs. "Oh, she's okay. She stopped me from driving when I was drunk," he said.

"*Drunk?*" the man exploded. "You idiot! You wanna get busted?" he cried.

Colin got to his feet and walked over to Nikki. "Hey, I'm sorry about all this. Uh—can I call you later?" he asked.

Nikki gave him one of the business cards she still had from the bank. She had blacked out her desk number and highlighted her home phone number. Then she hurried from the apartment without looking back.

Nikki was relieved to get in her car and head toward home. "Whew!" she said to herself. "Poor old Mr. Dempsey doesn't know the half of it. That guy who let himself into Colin's apartment looked like bad news—a loser and a creep for sure. I'll just bet he's a hardened criminal with a long rap sheet. If not,

26

I'm a really poor judge of character!"

But maybe that was *it*. Maybe that guy was Colin's partner in crime!

When Nikki got home, a message from Mr. Dempsey was waiting. He wanted her to meet with his *good* son, Dylan, right away. So Nikki called Dylan Dempsey at once.

"This is Nikki Peters. I'm working for your father. He thought it would be a good idea if we got together sometime today," she said.

"Oh, yeah, right. Dad told me about you. How about meeting for coffee and rolls tonight at Arbuckle's Coffee Shop. It's right off I-15. I usually stop there on my way home from work. Say about 6:30? That work for you?" Dylan said.

"That's fine," Nikki said. "In fact, it's quite close to where I live."

Nikki washed and dried her hair. As she did, she kept reminding herself of the promise Mr. Dempsey had made. After this investigative job was over, she would move up to management training at the mattress company. She'd get stock options and bonuses and everything! Soon she'd be earning *twice* what she had earned at the bank.

"Oh, well, if I can't find love, I might at least be making some money," Nikki thought to herself.

At about 4:30 that afternoon, Nikki's phone rang again.

"Hello—is this Ms. Peters?" The rich baritone voice sounded familiar.

"Yes, this is Nikki Peters," she said.

"This is Colin Dempsey," the voice said, now sounding totally sober. "Look, I just want to apologize for everything. You must think I'm the worst jerk in the world. I want to thank you for stopping me from driving. That was just so good of you. I'm really embarrassed that you had to get mixed up in my stupidity like that." He paused then and said, "I'm not *always* such a jerk."

"Oh, I'm sure you're not," Nikki said,

impressed by his apparent sincerity. Colin sounded like a different person. What an unexpected turnaround! Just when Nikki was ready to tell Mr. Dempsey that his worst fears about his son were probably true, here he was sounding so polite and friendly.

"I wouldn't blame you for telling me to drop dead," Colin went on. "But I'd sure appreciate it if you'd have breakfast with me tomorrow morning. I owe you, you know? So how about it? At least I can buy you a Belgian waffle with strawberries on top," Colin said.

Nikki was now feeling guilty about how quickly she had written the guy off. "Sure, I'd enjoy that," she said.

"Great! Then come over to Ozzie's Restaurant around 9:00 A.M., okay? I promise you won't see the moron you saw this morning," Colin said.

Nikki was smiling when she hung up. Her job would be a good bit easier if she could get closer to Colin. Maybe he was a good guy after all. At the moment there was no way to tell how things might turn out. *Anything* could happen. Nikki might even be the instrument that could eventually reunite father and son. That idea appealed to her very much.

Then Nikki searched her own heart, trying to be honest with herself. Colin was very handsome—and at the moment, charming. She had to guard against falling for him. The end of her relationship with Bart had been too sad and traumatic. She didn't want to get emotionally involved with anyone for a long, long time.

Nikki chose a new green business suit for her meeting with Dylan Dempsey. She arrived at Arbuckle's at almost the same moment he did. Nikki recognized him from the pictures she had seen of the Dempsey family. But Dylan had put on some weight since then, and it hadn't helped his appearance. She saw that he was also growing a large mustache like his father's. In fact he looked quite a bit like a young walrus.

Once they were seated, Dylan smiled at Nikki. "I understand you're going to help Dad get rid of the worst frustration in his life—my brother."

"Well, your father asked me to do some research and give him a complete report on Colin. He needs it so he can make some decisions about the future," Nikki said. "He wants to know what Colin is really doing with his life."

"*What* life?" Dylan sneered. Then the waitress came to take their order. Dylan looked over the menu and suggested cherry pastries with their coffee. Then he smirked and asked, "Well, Ms. Peters, have you met the fool yet?"

It wasn't hard to tell that there was no love lost between the brothers. The more Nikki talked to Dylan, the more she disliked him and sympathized with

Colin. "Well, yes, he and I have met—but I haven't really formed any definite opinions yet," she said.

Dylan looked disappointed. "Well, that surprises me. Most people who meet Colin are thoroughly revolted."

"Is that so? Well, your father has asked me for a balanced report. So I'm reserving any judgment until I have all the information I need," Nikki said.

"If you don't mind me asking," Dylan continued, "was he sober when you saw him? Colin's a drunkard on top of all his other faults, you know. If he was sober, then that's fortunate for you, because—"

"Actually, Mr. Dempsey," Nikki said coolly, "I'd rather not discuss this investigation—not with anyone but your father. For me to do otherwise would be unprofessional. So why don't you tell me whatever *you* think might be helpful in forming a conclusion."

Sighing impatiently, Dylan said, "Yes,

well, I've written down some of the bars he frequents. And I've listed the names of a few lowlife bums he hangs out with. If I were you I wouldn't get too close to them, though. Some of them are vicious criminals."

Nikki took the list and put it in her purse. "Thank you very much," she said.

"One of Colin's friends—a guy named Spike—he's a drug addict. He actually served time for attempted murder. If you ever see him, you'll never forget him. He was in a prison riot one time, and another thug hit him over the head with an axe," Dylan said.

Nikki said nothing. But now she knew the name of that frightful-looking man who came into the apartment.

"Ever since we were kids my father has had nothing but grief from Colin. My brother is ten years younger than I am, you know. We had different mothers," Dylan explained.

"Oh? I didn't know that," Nikki said.

"Oh, yeah. My parents were divorced when I was ten. Mom remarried and I got a great new stepdad. Then Dad married this showgirl—a trashy little gal named May. *She* was only 19 when Dad married her. Dad was 37 at the time. That girl was Colin's mother. She overdosed on drugs when Colin was six months old.

"A short time later Dad married again. A nice lady named Darlene. That's who he's with now. Colin never got along with her. And Darlene hates Colin as much as we all do. The fact is that Colin has been a thorn in everybody's side. You know—like the hateful kid in that old movie—he's a bad seed. That's what the guy is. Just a real bad seed."

Chapter 4

Nikki was starting to feel very sorry for Colin—in spite of what Dylan had intended. Now he stared across the table at Nikki. Detecting her sympathy for his brother, he became emotional.

"Ms. Peters, Colin is *unscrupulous*! We think he's been bilking old people with some bogus health food scheme. I could spend all day telling you the ugly things he's done to our family. If it weren't for his handsome face—and the charm he can put on if he wants—he would've been out on his backside a long time ago. But until now he's always weaseled second chances. I just hope this time will be different. And it *will*—if you give Dad the facts he needs to erase this hateful monster from our lives for good!"

Nikki didn't say a thing, but she considered Dylan's motives as she looked at him.

"Once Colin is disinherited," she thought to herself, "you get it *all*—isn't that right, buddy?"

For the next hour or so, Dylan recounted more of Colin's misadventures while Nikki listened politely.

Colin had clearly been a wild child. Not even a series of military academies had tamed him. He had destroyed furniture and plumbing and vandalized neighbor's homes. When Colin was 18, he'd gotten drunk and disrupted his father's birthday party for his wife. He'd even knocked down the white pavilion erected for the occasion. Finally, near the end of his long tirade, Dylan studied Nikki for her reaction.

"Well, I can see that he has certainly been a trial for you," Nikki said.

"Somehow my father has never gotten Colin out of his system. Dad puts on a good show—but I can tell that he's just itching to forgive the little creep one more time! He's hoping that you'll find that he has some redeeming features. But I assure you, Ms. Peters—there aren't any! Colin will con you, but deep down he's *evil*. Dad doesn't want to believe that he sired such a monster, but it's the truth," Dylan said.

"Well, thank you so much for your time, Mr. Dempsey," Nikki said. "You've filled in some important details for me." But Dylan's unbridled hatred of his brother tended to make her *more* rather than less sympathetic to Colin. It seemed to her that nobody could be *that* bad.

She thought Dylan's own greed was playing a big part in all this. Sure, there was easily enough Royal Mattress money to make *both* sons rich—but Dylan probably wanted it all. Maybe being a millionaire wasn't enough. Maybe he wanted to be a *billionaire*. After all, a whole loaf was better than half a loaf—

no matter how big the loaf might be!

Dylan Dempsey was silent for a few moments. Then his eyes narrowed, and he said bluntly, "Ms. Peters—you're not falling for him, are you?"

"*What?*" Nikki cried out indignantly. "Mr. Dempsey! I cannot tell you how insulted I am by that question!"

"You'd be surprised at how many women have fallen for my rotten brother. There's just something about him that's very appealing to women. Not only his looks—but that bad boy thing. When he was in high school and college, he had girls chasing him. I had to *work* to get dates. Not him. Chicks fell into his path like tenpins at the bowling alley," Dylan said bitterly.

Nikki looked straight into the man's pale eyes. "I am a professional woman who is doing a job for my employer. The ridiculous suggestion that I would become romantically involved with a client's son is offensive and stupid! As for what you've just told me, Mr. Dempsey, I cannot help but be surprised and a little shocked at the depths of your hatred for your own brother. I hardly know what to believe," she said.

"Yes, I *do* hate Colin. I admit it," Dylan said. "I've hated him for a long time—and with good reason."

Nikki finished her coffee and the waiter brought the bill. When Dylan appeared to be paying for her, she put up her hand. "No, thank you. I'm paying for my own," she insisted.

Nikki was glad that the meeting was over. She hadn't enjoyed being with Dylan Dempsey one bit.

"Just one more thing," Dylan said as they both got up.

"What?" Nikki asked.

"I guess you should know that he tried to kill me. Colin tried to kill me," Dylan said.

Chapter 5

"Pardon me?" Nikki gasped as she turned toward Dylan. "He *what*?"

"It's true. Dad invited him to come hunting with us last year. It was another of Dad's pathetic attempts to be 'family' again. Dad and I were hunting in the hills, and Colin was off by himself. The rifle shot only missed my head by *inches*, I'm telling you. Then Colin came out of the clearing, rifle in hand. He admitted he had fired it," Dylan said.

"But it was accidental, wasn't it?" Nikki asked. "Surely he didn't admit that he tried to kill you!"

"Not in so many words, no. But he sneered at me with *that look*, and I knew he was trying to kill me. I wanted Dad to call the police, but he wouldn't. He said he couldn't turn in his own son. I'm warning you, Ms. Peters—Colin is a very dangerous person. If you're smart, you won't ever forget that!" Dylan said.

A few minutes later Nikki was alone in her Corolla, driving up the freeway on-ramp. She thought Dylan's horror story must have been a lie—or at least a terrible exaggeration. After all, hunters accidentally shoot each other quite often. Surely that's what had really happened.

Nikki got home, showered, and slipped into her jogging clothes. Right behind her condo there was a fairly large wilderness area, a wildlife refuge. During her evening walks there, Nikki often saw rabbits, roadrunners, even coyotes. She had always loved to see the wild creatures. Running through the brushy open space gave her a sense of peace.

Nikki's thoughts turned to Bart Wheeler—about when he'd told her that he wasn't interested in marriage. After their relationship ended, Nikki had found her greatest peace in jogging through the wilderness. It had taken a long time to get over Bart.

The worst part of it was that Bart had her fooled so completely. She had helped him with his college tuition while he got his master's degree in business. All along, she'd foolishly taken it for granted that she was investing in their future together. She'd never doubted that he loved her as much as she loved him. She was so sure that he wanted a commitment as much as she did.

Then, suddenly, there was that awful conversation in Pasadena. They had driven there to see the Rose Parade on New Year's Day. The evening before, they'd gone out for dinner.

Nikki had been excited. She expected that this would be the night when he'd give her an engagement ring. But then he had given her a pearl necklace and said, "What's wrong with things as they are? Why do we need to be married?"

"But eventually we *will* be married—" Nikki had said uncertainly.

"Listen, Nikki. I guess the truth is that I don't really believe in marriage," Bart said. By the time the champagne corks were popping and everybody else was ringing in the New Year, Nikki was crying her heart out.

"Which proves," Nikki reminded herself as she jogged, "that you, girl, are not a perfect judge of people—so be careful." Maybe she was misjudging Colin, or even Dylan. It could be that her opinions were all wrong. She had to be very cautious. When she finally went to Mr. Dempsey with her report, she wanted to be absolutely sure it was as truthful as possible—uncolored by her own emotions.

A half moon appeared in the sky as Nikki jogged the trail. But it wasn't totally dark yet. Nikki could run her usual route in about 30 minutes. So she figured she still had time to get home before darkness settled in completely.

Ordinarily, nobody but Nikki was on the trail at this hour. The other walkers and joggers usually came out in the early morning before going to work. Nikki was not a morning person. Most of her energy came in the late afternoon and evening hours. But now, as she jogged along, she heard someone coming up behind her. She glanced back over her shoulder and saw a tall man in a pair of dark sweatpants and a T-shirt.

Nikki was surprised when a sudden chill of fear went up her spine. That wasn't like her. She wasn't an easily frightened person. Why, she'd gone skin diving off the coast of Mexico and shot the rapids in the western mountains! But getting mixed up in this investigation was something else. For some reason she definitely felt on edge now.

Nikki glanced back again. The man behind her seemed to be moving at the same pace that she was. He wasn't getting any closer. But it was too dark to see his face at all. That made Nikki nervous, so she increased her speed. Looking over her shoulder, she saw that he seemed to be coming faster, too!

Nikki was about to reach the most isolated part of the trail. Soon the path would enter a dense grove of big greasewood trees. If someone tried to jump her there, she'd be in serious trouble. Crying out for help wouldn't do her any good, either. She was still too far from the condos for anyone to hear her.

Nikki slipped her hand into her sweater pocket and quickly found the can of eye-irritating spray she always carried. Her hand was shaking as her thumb moved over the button. But she was prepared to let him have it if she had to.

Chapter 6

Nikki kept up her pace, dreading the path between the greasewood trees. When she looked back again, the man didn't seem to be gaining on her. Was he waiting for her to tire out? Maybe he thought she'd be easier to overtake if she slowed down. But *who* could be following her? Did her pursuer have anything to do with the Dempsey case? So far she hadn't done a thing to anger anybody.

"What have I gotten myself into?" she asked herself. "Why didn't I just stay at the bank job and watch my investments grow? As boring as the bank was, at least it was safe!"

Nikki ran on. She didn't realize that the tall dark figure was rapidly gaining on her. Then she heard him closing in fast. He was only about 20 feet back.

Nikki panicked. She knew she couldn't outrun him. The man was big and athletic, and he ran with a long stride. Most men could run faster than women anyway. So Nikki's hand closed on the spray can, and she slowed her pace, getting ready for the confrontation.

His voice reached her before he did. "You shouldn't be running on a lonely trail like this in the dark," the man said. "Don't you listen to TV or read the newspapers?"

Nikki stopped and turned, watching the tall man approach. If necessary, she wanted to be in position to blast him right in the face with her spray. But the nearer he came, the more harmless he seemed to be. He smiled as he slowed to a stop. "I hope I didn't scare you," he said politely. "But it really worries me when women jog out here alone at night. It's just not a good idea."

Nikki stared at his boyish face and crewcut hair. He wore a jacket with a Penn State logo. "Here I go again," Nikki thought to herself, "judging people on first impressions that are probably dead wrong."

Then she spoke out. "I always walk and jog here," she said cautiously. "I don't see any danger." Her hand was still in her pocket, ready to blast away if the man made any sudden moves toward her.

"My name is Ryan Kralik," he said. "I just moved into a condo over there." He pointed toward the condominiums where Nikki also lived. "I like to jog after work myself—but I'm a man. It's a different thing when you're a woman— especially a young woman as attractive as you are."

"It's good of you to be concerned— but I've never had any trouble," Nikki said, not volunteering her name.

"Well, maybe we'll bump into each

other again. Then you won't have to jog alone," Ryan Kralik said with a smile. Then he resumed his run and rapidly disappeared down the trail.

Nikki started running again, too—but slowly. She felt more comfortable with the strange man far ahead of her rather than trailing behind.

At the end of the trail was a loop and then the path toward home. Nikki finally wound up on the volleyball court near the condos. Ryan Kralik had beaten her home. He was now standing under the bright lights of the court. A dozen people were coming and going in the nearby parking lot.

Nikki finally relaxed. "Uh, my name is Nikki Peters," she said. "Thanks for the heads up about running at night. It would be nice to team up sometimes when we're jogging after work. For some reason I've never felt threatened—although I've run into a few rattlesnakes. But you're right. There are some pretty bad characters in this world. A girl really can't be too careful."

Ryan Kralik nodded. "Hi, Nikki," he said. "Rattlers tend to be more afraid of us than we are of them. With people it's different. I'll take a rattler any day."

Then they shook hands. Ryan seemed like a really nice fellow. Nikki liked him. He looked like an ordinary young guy, the kind you'd meet in a college classroom. And she thought it was sweet that he was worried about a girl he didn't even know.

Before going to sleep that night, Nikki read some more of the file material about Colin Dempsey. He had a high IQ, but his intelligence was never reflected in his grades or on the job. During his brief military career, he had flunked almost everything—but he had qualified as an expert on the rifle range.

Chapter 7

Nikki woke up early the next day. For some reason, she was nervous about her breakfast with Colin Dempsey. But she shook it off and quickly dressed in a dark pullover sweater and a pair of slacks. Then she headed out. Ozzie's was a middle-class restaurant on the edge of the downtown business district. She hadn't eaten there before. Someone had told her that it was okay, but not a *fine* restaurant by any standards.

Nikki was in the restaurant about ten minutes before Colin showed up. For a moment, she wondered if he might be drunk again and had forgotten all about their appointment. But then he came hurrying in the door and rushed over to the booth where she sat. "Sorry I'm so late!" he said. Nikki was already drinking her second cup of coffee. "I had trouble starting my car," he added with an apologetic smile. "I had to get a friend to jump-start it." He picked up the menu. "The omelet here is pretty good." He must have forgotten about the Belgian waffle he offered to buy.

Nikki smiled and ordered an omelet.

"I was really an idiot yesterday," Colin said. "And I want to thank you for coming here this morning. In your place, I'm not sure I would have."

"Don't worry about it. Everybody makes mistakes," Nikki said.

"I don't know what got into me yesterday," Colin said. "I usually don't drink that much—*never* that early in the morning! It was really stupid. I'm sure glad you showed up and got me out of that driver's seat," Colin said.

"Well, like I said, a drunk driver killed my father when I was a little girl. So when I saw you, I felt that I had to do something. It makes me angry when people try to drive when they aren't able to do it safely," Nikki said.

"You're right. *Of course* you're right. And I'm not going to deny that I do have a drinking problem. It's true—I drink too much. And I've got to get my act together. I know that," Colin said, sounding very reasonable.

"You could try AA," Nikki said. "It's worked for several people I know."

Colin nodded, took a gulp of coffee, and looked in Nikki's eyes.

"So, do you work somewhere in my neighborhood?" he asked.

"No, I work at a bank downtown," Nikki said. "Most mornings I pass right by your apartment on my way there." Nikki certainly wasn't going to tell Colin Dempsey her real reason for being near his apartment that morning.

"Married?" he asked with a smile.

"No," Nikki said. It was none of his business, of course. But she didn't want to antagonize him by saying so. Then the waiter delivered two omelets. And they looked delicious—fluffy and rich with melted cheese and chunks of sausage.

"Maybe the fates tossed us together, eh?" Colin said with a flirtatious grin. Nikki was reminded that Colin liked to "collect" pretty girls.

"You seem like a really sharp young woman," Colin said. "And you are certainly beautiful. You must think I'm a big loser the way I acted yesterday."

"I don't know anything about you, really," Nikki lied. "It's foolish to judge someone by one incident."

He gave out a shallow laugh. "Looking at me now, and knowing where I live, it may be hard to believe— but I grew up in a rich man's house. I've been to Europe half a dozen times. I've hiked the Alps with my father. Thanks to my father's connections, I've met two presidents and a prime minister. But I'm sort of the black sheep of the family now. Have you ever heard of Royal Mattresses?" he asked.

"Oh, yes, sure. They're supposed to be the best. I see their commercials all the time on TV," Nikki said.

"Well, my dad started that company and built it up into a big multinational operation. I could be working in the business right now. Yeah, I *could* be living the good life," Colin said, shaking his head.

Nikki slowly ate her omelet. He was right about the food here. It was very tasty. "So why aren't you doing that?" she asked him in a mildly interested voice. She didn't want to seem too curious.

"Because my dad has always hated me," Colin said.

"Wow, that's a pretty terrible thing to say," Nikki said. "Fathers don't usually hate their own sons for no reason at all."

"My dad hated me all my life. He still does. My mom died when I was very young—and right away Dad started looking for wife number three. He stuck me away in a boarding school. Even for a little kid, it wasn't hard to get the picture. He wanted me to just kinda disappear and not complicate his life. But I got sick of being ignored. I got sick of a father who didn't even want me home for school vacations. I guess I caused a little trouble to get attention. It didn't work out the way I hoped it would, though. So the more he ignored me, the more I rebelled. But then he hated me even more," Colin said.

"But didn't you say you hiked the Alps with your father?" Nikki asked.

"Yeah, there was that one trip. But he was on my case the whole time. I think he would have liked it if I'd fallen off the mountain and broken my neck," Colin said bitterly.

"You sound really angry about your childhood," Nikki said. She watched Colin closely to gauge his reaction.

"I think *anybody* in my situation would have plenty to be angry about," Colin said. "My father lavished all his love and attention on my putrid brother—a slob of a man. I was the outsider. I've *always* been on the outside looking in." Nikki could see the handsome contours of his face harden in the sunlight streaming through the window. "Now I'm scrounging for every dime, and my brother is living off the family fortune."

"Have you—uh—ever tried to heal the differences you have with your father?" Nikki asked.

Colin sneered. "That's impossible. He won't even *talk* to me! Nothing in this world would make him happier than to hear that I've been run over by an eighteen-wheeler. Oh, yeah—he'd be delighted to know that I was out of his life for good," he said.

"Oh, that's really a terrible thing to say!" Nikki said. "I'm sure it's not true."

Chapter 8

"You don't know my father," Colin insisted. "He's a greedy, selfish, vile man." But then the expression on Colin's face suddenly changed. Now he looked embarrassed. "But why am I burdening you with the dreary details of my miserable life? You must think I'm a self-centered jerk. May I call you Nikki?"

"Sure," Nikki said as she finished her omelet and put down her fork.

"Okay, Nikki, what about you? You said you lost your dad when you were young. So I guess we're both orphans in a way. I lost my mom when I was very small. It seems like you've handled that better than I have. You seem so—I don't know—so well-adjusted. You said you weren't married. But I bet you have a steady boyfriend. What a lucky stiff he is!" Colin smiled.

Nikki thought he was probably fishing—trying to find out if she was available. That was a bit childish, but it didn't make him evil. Maybe he was just looking for some company.

"Actually I'm pretty busy with my career. I haven't got enough time for much of a social life," Nikki said. "My job really keeps me going."

"Oh, well, thanks for taking the time to meet me here. I really wanted the chance to apologize for the stuff I got you into," Colin said. He continued to look at Nikki with interest.

Again, Nikki noticed that he was a very handsome young man. She had to admit that his looks disarmed her. And he had sort of a hurt-little-boy charm to him, too. It certainly was *possible* that people had wronged him. Maybe he really *was* a victim of forces beyond his control. At least that was the picture he painted. For now, Nikki was willing to buy most of it—but she forced herself to be cautious. She remembered all the horrible things that Dylan had said. If even half of them were true, Colin was a hardcore loser.

"I'm sorry you're not getting along with your family. So tell me—what are your plans for going to school or doing something to get your own career going?" Nikki asked. "These days, it's hard to get very far without college."

"Oh, I've been to college," Colin said. "I couldn't concentrate, though. My father insisted that I work my way through—even though he had plenty of money to pay for my education. It was hard to balance my two-bit jobs and keep my grades up at the same time. It just didn't work. I almost had a breakdown. And then I was going with a girl I really cared about. But that broke up, and I was totally bummed. So a lot of heavy stuff just kept piling up on me.

I guess I just couldn't take it."

"You could go back to college *now*," Nikki said. "You're still a young guy."

"I guess I could," he said, without much enthusiasm. "I don't know. I've been told for so many years that I'm no good, I've sort of begun to believe it. You know, Nikki, it's been ages since I've talked to anybody the way I've been talking to you. I don't mean to be dumping on you like this, but—"

Again, Nikki felt sorry for him. But she was fighting emotional involvement. She wanted to be absolutely honest with Mr. Dempsey. Deep in her heart she wanted to honestly tell the father that his son *could* be salvaged. She would really love to write that in her report—to play an important part in mending a badly broken family.

And Nikki liked Colin in spite of herself. She didn't *want* to—but she did. "Colin," she said, "people can do pretty much anything that they really want to do. If you make a decision to go back to college—and you were willing to work really hard—you could make it. In a few years you could graduate and get a really good job. Wouldn't it feel great to prove to your family that they were all wrong about you?"

Colin smiled. His big brown eyes sparkled and seemed to light up his face. "You're wonderful, Nikki! Here you meet this jerk who is too drunk to even drive a car—and all of a sudden you're giving him a new lease on life! I wish I hadn't ruined my chances with you in the beginning. But you've seen me at my worst. I wouldn't blame you for wanting to avoid me." But even as he spoke, there was hope in his voice. He was wishing that Nikki would tell him he hadn't destroyed his chances for a relationship with her.

But Nikki couldn't go that far. Not yet anyway. Maybe later, when this job was over. But even then it would be awkward to work for Mr. Dempsey and date his son—the bad seed. Unless, of course, Nikki managed to reconcile the family. She smiled at Colin and said, "Well, who can tell? Never say *never* about anything."

Colin looked pleased. "I'd sure like to get to know you better, Nikki. Would it be okay if I called you sometime? Maybe we could go out—" he said.

"I guess that would be okay," Nikki said. After all, in order to do her job she needed to stay fairly close to this man. It was her duty to find out as much as she could about him.

"Great!" Colin said, grasping Nikki's hand and giving it a squeeze. "Did I tell you that you're the most wonderful girl I've ever met, Nikki? I *should* have said that—because you are! I haven't been so hopeful about myself in years. Thanks to *you*, Nikki. *You* did that for me."

Chapter 9

Nikki felt pretty hopeful. Maybe Colin really *could* clean up his act. This assignment from Mr. Dempsey might have a happy ending after all. It might turn out to be win-win. Didn't Dylan say that his father was secretly hoping to let Colin back into his life? Of course Dylan wouldn't be thrilled if he had to share the inheritance—but that didn't bother Nikki at all.

About mid-day, Nikki got a phone call from Dylan Dempsey. "So how is the project for my father going, Ms. Peters?" he asked.

Nikki couldn't help resenting the inquiry. "Why, everything is just fine, Mr. Dempsey," she said briskly.

"No—I mean, have you reached any

conclusions about my brother?" Dylan asked in a pushy, nervous voice.

"Mr. Dempsey, I believe we went over this already. I'm looking into this matter for your *father*. He's the only one I report to," Nikki said.

There was a long silence on the other end of the line. Then Dylan snarled, "You're already on *his* side, aren't you?"

"Excuse me, Mr. Dempsey. I'm very busy," Nikki said.

"I knew it! Father is *stupid*. I told him to hire a professional investigator to get the dirt on Colin. But no. He had the screwball idea that a hot babe could get at the truth faster," Dylan fumed. "Now the same thing has happened to you that happens to every dumb chick. You've fallen for Colin, haven't you? You're blind to what he really is."

"Goodbye, Mr. Dempsey," Nikki said as she hung up. Dylan was obviously terrified that Colin might be allowed back into the family's good graces. The very idea was making him hysterical.

Nikki checked some of the sources Dylan had given her. The last time Colin had talked to his father, he'd claimed to be working as a security guard. But when Nikki checked it out, she found that he'd never worked at that company.

Then Nikki found another name and address. It was an 80-year-old woman whose son was outraged that his mother had purchased $150.00 worth of herbal remedies from Colin Dempsey. When Nikki called the elderly woman, she seemed quite pleased with her herbal supplements. But her son was still convinced that his mother had been bilked. Nikki wondered if Colin had worked his charms on the elderly woman.

Maybe Colin *was* a born con man. Or maybe he peddled fake herbal remedies out of sheer desperation for money.

In the early evening, Nikki went out jogging as usual. She didn't see Ryan Kralik until she was well under way.

Then there he was, jogging behind her. Nikki slowed until he caught up.

"Beautiful evening, isn't it?" Nikki said. "The moon looks huge tonight."

"Yeah—spectacular. And you can see Venus, too," Ryan said.

"Wow," Nikki thought, "this guy must be into astronomy." She looked up and smiled at him. "Are you a scientist or something?" she asked.

"Nah, I'm a high school teacher. But I really love science and especially astronomy. My job is to get 130 kids as excited about the planets as they are about the newest video game," he said, laughing. "It's a lost cause, I guess. But it's fun trying. I wasn't always a teacher. I used to be a cop—for two years."

They had walked about ten yards when a rifle shot cracked the air. Ryan grabbed Nikki by the arm and pulled her down beside him in the brush along the side of the path.

"Man!" Ryan gasped. "I didn't think

I had any enemies who were *that* mad! But that was too close for comfort."

Nikki gulped. "Maybe it was meant for me," she blurted out.

It flashed through her mind that maybe Dylan was behind it. She knew he didn't want her to present Colin in a good light to her boss. But was he so determined to stop her that he'd hire a hitman to take her out?

Or was it Colin? Was he trying to shoot her "accidentally"—the way he had supposedly tried to shoot his brother? But *why*? As far as she knew, she was on good terms with Colin.

"Come on, let's get back home and call the police," Ryan said, interrupting Nikki's thoughts. He walked beside her protectively, keeping her close to the trees. Ryan wasn't a bit sure who the shooter was after. But he wanted to make sure the gunman wouldn't have another clear shot.

Chapter 10

In minutes, the police arrived at Nikki's condo. She told them about the work she was doing for Mr. Dempsey. Then Nikki took the police officers to the spot where the rifle shot had almost hit her. They started to search for the rifle shell and were still combing the brush when Nikki went home.

She was shaken. She'd already made up her mind to quit the job. It wasn't worth sacrificing her life for.

Ryan Kralik was waiting for her in the community recreation room. They talked and drank decaf coffee for half an hour or so. It helped to calm her down. He seemed to be a really nice guy. The fact that his condo was just a few doors from hers was very comforting. Having an ex-cop for a neighbor made her feel a whole lot safer.

Nikki couldn't sleep that night. She kept thinking of a shadowy figure standing on the knoll overlooking the hiking trail. He had actually fired a rifle at her! It was a difficult shot because of all the trees and the shadows. She remembered that Colin had been an expert marksman in the army. But Nikki had no reason to believe that Dylan had ever fired a rifle.

And yet—what possible reason would Colin have to harm her? After all, he had flirted with her and hinted that he wanted to date her! And she hadn't turned him down.

At nine the next morning, Colin Dempsey called Nikki.

"Are you okay?" he asked.

"Yes," Nikki said.

"The police talked to me last night. They said that somebody shot at you. I was just *sick* when I heard about what happened! I can't imagine why anybody in this world would shoot at a great girl like you. What's going on, Nikki?" Colin said in a very upset voice.

Nikki thought about what the police might have told Colin. Had they told him that she was an investigator for his father? She had asked them not to reveal that information. And they'd agreed that telling him would place her at more risk.

"Maybe the rifleman wasn't aiming at me. Maybe it was just a random shot," Nikki said.

"I guess they talked to me—the police, I mean—because they're talking to all your friends," Colin said.

"I suppose. They wanted the names and addresses of everyone I've been in contact with over the past month. They hoped someone might be able to give them a piece of information that would turn out to be useful," Nikki said.

"I was glad to talk to them—but I'm afraid I wasn't much help. Man, Nikki,

I'm so worried about you," Colin said. "Would you like me to come over just in case something else happens? After all you've done for me, I'd be glad to do anything!"

"No, thanks, I'm fine," Nikki said.

But that night, just as Nikki was about to start her run, Colin Dempsey showed up. "I got your address off the Internet since you didn't invite me," he said in a cold voice. "I wanted to talk to you about a call I got from my brother yesterday morning. He told me who you really are. What an actress you are! You sure had me fooled. It was a bummer to find out that you're just a dirty little snake like all the rest of them. You've been trying to get the goods on me so I never get any of the old man's money."

Nikki froze. So Dylan had told Colin the truth about who she was. That made sense. It was his way of ending her role as an investigator. Dylan was terrified that she was on Colin's side—but he wasn't about to tell his brother that.

"I've been wondering how to get rid of you ever since," Colin said in an icy voice. The look in his eyes was deadly. "It was me who tried to shoot you last night. You had no idea, did you? But I don't have a weapon with me now—so I guess I'll have to strangle you."

Then they both heard a slight rustling in the bushes, and Ryan Kralik stood up. "Hold it, mister!" he growled. "I've got a gun, and it's loaded." Ryan walked out of the brush where he'd been hiding— just in case something happened.

The police came within minutes. After they took Colin Dempsey away, Nikki and Ryan went to a neighborhood restaurant for a quiet dinner. She told him all about her job.

"You swam with sharks, Nikki, and one almost ate you," Ryan said.

"Luckily, I had a shark-buster on my team," Nikki said with a grateful smile.

She could see the ocean from the

window of the restaurant. The moon was spilling a beautiful milky glow over the water. Ryan covered Nikki's hand with his own. For the first time in months, Nikki felt that something wonderful really could happen after all.

COMPREHENSION QUESTIONS

RECALL

1. Why did Nikki Peters feel she had to leave her job at the bank?

2. How did Dylan Dempsey feel about his brother?

3. What kind of product did Colin Dempsey sell to old people?

WHO AND WHERE?

1. Where did Nikki meet Ryan Kralik?

2. Which character reminded Nikki of a big old walrus?

3. Which Dempsey son was *less* attractive to Nikki?

DRAWING CONCLUSIONS

1. Why did Hal Dempsey think Nikki was the best job applicant?

2. Why did Colin Dempsey apologize to Nikki?

3. Why did Dylan conclude that Nikki was falling in love with Colin?

VOCABULARY

1. Mr. Dempsey described his son Colin as a "wastrel." What is a *wastrel*?

2. Dylan said that his brother was "unscrupulous." What does *unscrupulous* mean?

3. Nikki was careful not to "antagonize" Colin Dempsey. What does *antagonize* mean?